NOTHING
CAN POSSIBLY GO
WRONG

D1113473

NOTHING
CAN POSSIBLY GO
WRONG

written by **PRUDENCE SHEN**
art by **FAITH ERIN HICKS**
colors by **ALISON ACTON**

:01
First Second
New York

First Second
New York

Published by First Second
First Second is an imprint of Roaring Brook Press, a division of Holtzbrinck Publishing Holdings Limited Partnership
120 Broadway, New York, NY 10271
firstsecondbooks.com

Library of Congress Control Number: 2020919587

Our books may be purchased in bulk for promotional, educational, or business use. Please contact your local
bookseller or the Macmillan Corporate and Premium Sales Department at (800) 221-7945 ext. 5442 or by email at
MacmillanSpecialMarkets@macmillan.com.

First edition, 2013
Revised edition, 2021
Edited by Calista Brill and Kiara Valdez
Cover design by Kirk Benshoff
Interior book design by Colleen AF Venable and Sunny Lee
Colors by Alison Acton

Nothing Can Possibly Go Wrong was drawn with light blue Col-erase pencils on Bristol paper and inked with a
Raphael Kolinsky watercolor brush, and colored in Photoshop.

Printed in China by 1010 Printing International Limited, North Point, Hong Kong

ISBN 978-1-250-77961-8 (paperback)
10 9 8 7 6 5 4 3 2 1

ISBN 978-1-250-77962-5 (hardcover)
10 9 8 7 6 5 4 3 2 1

Don't miss your next favorite book from First Second! For the latest updates go to firstsecondnewsletter.com and sign
up for our enewsletter.

For my parents,
even though they never bought me a robot
—P. S.

For all the girl geeks
—F. E. H.

YOU'RE JUST LUCKY I CAME TO PICK YOU UP AT ALL—

—AFTER WHAT YOUR GIRLFRIEND AND HER JACKAL CHEERLEADERS DID TO ME.

HOLLY'S NOT MY GIRLFRIEND ANYMOOOOOOORRE—

SCREEEE

OHGODLAMPPOST!

WHAT DO YOU MEAN SHE'S NOT YOUR GIRLFRIEND ANYMORE?? YOU'RE THE CAPTAIN OF THE BASKETBALL TEAM. SHE'S HEAD CHEERLEADER!

IT'S AN IRON-CLAD HIGH SCHOOL RULE YOU DATE HOLLY.

TO MAKE THE REST OF US LESS-ATTRACTIVE-BUT-INFINITELY-SMARTER MORTALS HATE YOU.

SORRY. NOT MY GIRLFRIEND ANYMORE.

HUH.

DID SHE GIVE YOU A REASON?

NOPE. THREE WEEKS AGO SHE DECIDED WE WERE DATING, AND NOW WE'RE NOT. HOLLY MOVES IN MYSTERIOUS WAYS.

FWIP

WELL, WHATEVER! DO YOU KNOW WHAT YOUR NOW EX-GIRLFRIEND DID? SHE'S TRYING TO TAKE MY SCIENCE TEAM'S FUNDING TO BUY UNIFORMS FOR HER EVIL CHEER SQUAD, THAT'S WHAT!

SO PRINCIPAL GETTY CALLS ME TO HER OFFICE TODAY AND I'M THINKING "WELL, CRAP, THE PHYSICS LAB HAD TO CATCH ON EVENTUALLY," RIGHT?

NO! IT'S HOLLY AND HER EVIL FEMBOT CO-CAPTAIN NORA, ASKING TO SPEND MY ROBOTICS COMPETITION MONEY ON THEIR NEW HOOCHIE OUTFITS.

YOU DIDN'T SAY THAT TO HER, DID YOU? BECAUSE SHE PUNCHES.

HARD.

GETTY DECIDED THAT SINCE THE MONEY HADN'T TECHNICALLY BEEN EARMARKED FOR THE SCIENCE TEAM, SHE'D LET THE STUDENT COUNCIL DECIDE WHO GOT TO SPEND IT.

THAT'S GOOD, RIGHT?

I CAN'T KNOW FOR SURE IF A PRESTIGIOUS NATIONAL ROBOTICS COMPETITION IS GOING TO BE HIGHER ON THE STUDENT COUNCIL'S AGENDA THAN CHEERLEADING UNIFORMS.

SCRREEE

IT'S A RISK I CAN'T TAKE.

WHAT ARE YOU PLANNING?

NOTHING . . . *BAD.*

I DON'T BELIEVE—OH GOD, LOOK OUT FOR THAT SEMI!

TRUST ME, CHARLES, I HAVE THIS WELL IN HAND.

BEEP! EEEEEEP

OH, THANK GOD.

SCREECH

IF YOU'RE SO SCARED TO RIDE WITH ME, YOU SHOULD DRIVE YOURSELF TO SCHOOL.

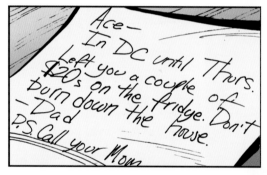

Ace—
In DC until Thurs.
Left you a couple of
$20s on the fridge. Don't
burn down the house.
—Dad
P.S. Call your Mom

—Dad
Call your Mom.

YEAH,
THAT'S NOT
HAPPENING.

AND THAT'S MY BRILLIANT PLAN.

NATE—YOU'RE TRYING TO RUN FOR STUDENT BODY PRESIDENT! *YOU'RE LITERALLY TRYING TO WIN A POPULARITY CONTEST!*

OF COURSE I CARE ABOUT GOING TO THE COMPETITION, BUT WHO'S GOING TO VOTE FOR YOU FOR STUDENT BODY PRESIDENT?

I'M PRESIDENT OF THE ROBOTICS TEAM, SO YOU GUYS WILL.

THE FUTURE!

NATE, *NO ONE* BESIDES US IS GOING TO VOTE FOR YOU.

THAT IS WHERE YOU'D BE WRONG. I'VE ALREADY SCOUTED OUT THE CANDIDATE POOL.

ALL THE PEOPLE RUNNING FOR STUDENT BODY PRESIDENT THIS YEAR HAVE EVEN LESS SOCIAL STATUS THAN ME.

IS THAT EVEN POSSIBLE?

SHUT UP, BEN.

THE POINT IS, I'D BE RUNNING AGAINST PEOPLE IN THE CHESS CLUB, AND THEY'RE EVEN LESS POPULAR THAN WE ARE.

GEEZ, NATE, I'M SURE INSULTING YOUR VOTING CONSTITUENCY IS A GREAT CAMPAIGN STRATEGY.

I CAN WIN THIS THING.

NO, YOU CAN'T.

17

GUYS, I CAN HEAR YOU SCREECHING FROM THE STREET.

WE WERE HAVING A REASONED DISCUSSION ABOUT OUR REVENUE STREAM.

AND YOU'RE LATE, JOANNA.

PLEASE, EVERYBODY IS ALWAYS LATE.

AND HOW IS OUR BABY TODAY?

JUST A HEADS UP: I'M GOING TO RUN FOR STUDENT BODY PRESIDENT.

YEAH, SURE YOU ARE.

LOOK, THERE'S ONLY SEVEN MONTHS UNTIL THE NATIONAL COMPETITION. WE HAVE THE BEST MACHINE OF THE BUNCH—

YES WE DO. YOU'RE THE MEANEST, FASTEST—

—AND WE DESERVE THE CHANCE TO RUB THE OTHER TEAMS' FACES IN IT.

AND IF RUNNING FOR STUDENT BODY PRESIDENT IS WHAT'S GOING TO GET US THERE, I'M WILLING TO TAKE ONE FOR THE TEAM.

ARE YOU SERIOUS ABOUT RUNNING?

WHAT'S WRONG WITH YOU GUYS? WHERE'S ALL THIS DOUBT COMING FROM?

FROM REALITY.

IT'S NOT MY JOB TO BE REALISTIC! IT'S MY JOB TO BE VISIONARY!

MY VISION IS WHY I'M PRESIDENT OF THE ROBOTICS CLUB!

ACTUALLY, WE MADE YOU PRESIDENT BECAUSE YOUR PARENTS LET US WORK IN YOUR BASEMENT.

MEETING CANCELLED! GET OUT OF MY BASEMENT!

HOLLY'S GONNA
BE MAAAD
ABOUT THIS.

WHAT THE HELL IS THIS??

I'VE ALWAYS HAD POLITICAL ASPIRATIONS.

COUGH.

?

VOTE NATE HARDING FOR STUDENT BODY PRESIDENT

VOTE NATE HARDING FOR STUDENT BODY PRESIDENT

UM, HEY...?

OW! YOU REALIZE I HAVE A SPINE, RIGHT?

I KNEW SOMETHING WAS UP YESTERDAY! DIDN'T YOU LEARN ANYTHING FROM MY TWELFTH BIRTHDAY INCIDENT?

I ONLY RENTED THAT PONY TO MAKE YOU HAPPY.

I CAN'T BELIEVE YOU.

LET'S STOP PRETENDING THAT YOU CARE ABOUT ME RUNNING FOR STUDENT BODY PRESIDENT—

OR THAT YOU CARE ABOUT THE CHEERLEADERS GETTING THEIR UNIFORMS.

NATE, SHHH!

YOU ARE SUCH A WUSS. THEY'RE CHEERLEADERS, NOT THE KGB.

YOU DON'T EVEN *KNOW*.

WHAT DON'T I KNOW? SERIOUSLY, WHAT?

SHE KNOWS I KNOW YOU. SHE'S GOING TO BLAME ME BECAUSE I KNOW YOU.

WHAT?? THAT DOESN'T MAKE ANY SENSE!

YOU DON'T EVEN KNOW.

FWIP

THMP THMP THMP

WHAT THE HELL JUST HAPPENED?

IS CHARLIE NOLAN SERIOUSLY AFRAID OF THE CHEERLEADERS?

HI?

CHARLES, WE HAVE THINGS TO DISCUSS.

OH?

WSSH WHOOSH

NEWS HAS COME TO US REGARDING THE STUDENT BODY ELECTIONS, CHARLES.

NORA AND I HAVE CERTAIN SOURCES.

THEY HAVE SOURCES.

OUR SOURCES INFORM US THAT THE DISCRETIONARY FUNDS WITH WHICH WE INTEND TO BUY NEW CHEERLEADING UNIFORMS ARE TO BE ENTRUSTED TO THE STUDENT COUNCIL.

THIS WOULD EXPLAIN–

–WHY YOUR LITTLE FRIEND NATE HARDING IS SUDDENLY RUNNING FOR STUDENT BODY PRESIDENT, WOULDN'T IT, CHARLES?

POSSIBLY?

YOU DO WANT THE SQUAD TO HAVE NEW UNIFORMS, DON'T YOU?

TO DEFEAT OUR COMPETITORS AT THE NATIONAL CHEERLEADING CHAMPIONSHIP AND PREVENT ME FROM HAVING TO MURDER YOU IN YOUR SLEEP FOR NOT INFORMING US OF NATE HARDING'S LITTLE PLAN?

YES?

GOOD.

I DON'T UNDERSTAND.

YOU'RE RUNNING FOR STUDENT BODY PRESIDENT, CHARLES.

YOU'RE GOING TO BEAT NATE HARDING IN THE ELECTION AND MAKE SURE WE GET THE FUNDING WE NEED FOR OUR NEW UNIFORMS.

WH-WHAT?? BUT I—

WE DISCUSSED THE POSSIBILITY OF RUNNING A CHEERLEADER IN THE ELECTION, BUT WE'RE IN TRAINING FOR NATIONALS AND CAN'T RISK DISTRACTION.

YOU WERE OUR ONLY OPTION.

I'VE SENT TWO JV MEMBERS TO REGISTER YOU OFFICIALLY WITH THE PRINCIPAL'S OFFICE, AND YOUR CAMPAIGN BEGINS TOMORROW . . .

. . . BRIGHT AND EARLY.

YOU'D BETTER APPRECIATE ALL THE TIME AND ENERGY WE'RE SINKING INTO YOUR VICTORY, NOLAN.

WHAT WAS THAT ABOUT? HOLLY DECIDE SHE WANT YOU BACK?

NO, AND I DON'T WANT TO TALK ABOUT IT.

SUIT YOURSELF, CHIEF.

WHAT'RE YOU GUYS DOING STILL STANDING AROUND? IT'S PRACTICE!

WE'VE GOT A GAME AGAINST WEST ON THURSDAY, FOLKS!

WHAP

NOLAN!

FOCUS ON THE *GAME!* YOU'RE TEAM CAPTAIN!

NOW ACT LIKE ONE.

SORRY, COACH.

"SORRY, COACH."

SHUT UP, BRENDAN.

AYE, AYE, CAPTAIN.

FWUMP

OH HEY, HERE THEY COME.

I WISH THEY WEREN'T SO TERRIFYING.

BUT THEN YOU'D THINK THEY WERE LESS HOT.

TRUE.

Psshh

PASTA

BRRRING

CRAP.

SSHHH

HELLO?

HI, CHARLIE.

HI, DAD. DO YOU KNOW WHERE THE TOMATO SAUCE IS?

WE HAVE TOMATO SAUCE?

YES, DAD, WE HAVE TOMATO SAUCE . . . SOMEWHERE.

SO HOW WAS SCHOOL?

SCHOOL WAS SCHOOL, EXCEPT APPARENTLY NATE'S RUNNING FOR STUDENT BODY PRESIDENT.

NATE HARDING? KID DOWN THE STREET?

YEP. I CAN'T BELIEVE YOU USED TO MAKE ME PLAY WITH HIM.

YEAH, WELL, HIS PARENTS THOUGHT HE'D TURN OUT WEIRD.

HE DID, JUST NOT THE WAY YOU THOUGHT HE WOULD.

I BET THERE'S MORE TO THIS STORY. TELL YOU WHAT, WHEN I GET BACK NEXT WEEK, WHY DON'T WE TAKE A WEEKEND TO GO CAMPING, JUST THE TWO OF US.

YOU CAN TELL ME ALL ABOUT IT THEN.

REALLY, DAD, IT'S OKAY.

WELL, I HAVE A DINNER MEETING, SO I'D BETTER RUN. YOU OKAY AT HOME?

YEAH, EVERYTHING'S FINE.

CALL YOUR MOM.

BYE, DAD.

PSSHHH

45

NATE & CHARLIE'S PLAYDATE

SHE HAS A BOYFRIEND NAMED TIM.

I HEAR YOU, UH, PLAY BASKETBALL?

YEAH!

I'VE NEVER KNOWN WHAT'S SO GREAT ABOUT IT.

IT'S ONLY THE BEST GAME IN THE WORLD.

I LIKE ROBOTS.

"I'M GOING TO BUILD A ROBOT SOMEDAY."

BZZZT

HELLO?

REMEMBER HOW YOU SAID THE CHEERLEADERS WEREN'T THE KGB?

YES. BECAUSE THEY AREN'T.

49

WSST

TOSS

THEY ARE, NATE.

THEY *ARE.*

CHARLIE, BREATHE. I HARDLY THINK THE POM-POM GESTAPO CAN DO ANYTHING TO YOU.

THEY CAN FORCE ME INTO THE ELECTION.

OH, *SURE.*

I'M NOT KIDDING, NATE! THEY CAME UP TO ME YESTERDAY BEFORE PRACTICE AND SAID THEY'D REGISTERED ME FOR THE ELECTION!

STOP FREAKING OUT. IT'S NOT LIKE THEY CAN MAKE YOU CAMPAIGN.

HOW DO YOU KNOW THEY CAN'T MAKE ME CAMPAIGN? PEOPLE MAKE ME DO STUFF ALL THE TIME. REMEMBER WHEN YOU MADE ME TAKE YOUR COUSIN TO HER DANCE?

YES, BUT NOW YOU'RE OLDER AND HAVE SINCE GROWN A PAIR, RIGHT?

AND ANYWAY, I'M SURE THEY CAN'T ACTUALLY MAKE YOU RUN IF YOU DON'T WANT TO.

YES, THEY CAN.

THE POINT IS, IT DOESN'T MATTER IF THEY DID THE PAPERWORK FOR YOU, YOU AREN'T GOING TO CAMPAIGN.

ARE YOU?

NO, BUT *STILL*.

CHARLIE.
ARE YOU?

NO, NATE,
I AM NOT
CAMPAIGNING.

IT'LL BE AS
IF I WASN'T
EVEN IN THE
RACE.

GOOD.

YOU.

ME?

HEY, MAN, THANKS FOR THE CANDY.

YOU TOTALLY GOT MY VOTE, NOLAN.

FWIP

THIS ISN'T MY FAULT.

I WILL *KILL* AND *EAT YOU.*

BUT YOU'RE LACTOSE INTOLERANT! I HAD MILK THIS MORNING!

I'LL RISK IT!

NATE, YOU'RE GOING TO BE LATE FOR FIRST PERIOD!

THMP THMP THMP THMP

THMP

TRIP

WSST

WHUMP

OOF.

VOTE NOLAN

VOTE NOLAN

SO WHEN THE CHEERLEADERS TRIPPED YOU, DID YOU GET TO TOUCH ANY OF THEM?

THEIR . . . *SKIN?*

KNOCK IT OFF, YOU TWO.

SMACK WHAP

59

WE HAVE A RULE ABOUT COMMENTS LIKE THOSE. DON'T WE HAVE A RULE?

WE'RE NOT ALLOWED TO MAKE THEM.

EXACTLY.

NATE, CHARLIE NOLAN IS THE SCHOOL'S OFFICIAL BENEVOLENT JOCK. EVERYONE LIKES HIM.

FLIP FLIP

YOU CAN'T BEAT SOMEONE LIKE THAT IN AN ELECTION. WHAT'RE YOU GOING TO DO?

FUNNY YOU SHOULD ASK.

MASTER PLAN!!

LOOK, CHARLIE—

I'M SORRY I HAD TO DO SUCH A ROTTEN THING, BUT THE ROBOTICS CLUB MADE IT CLEAR YOU ARE POPULAR AND I AM NOT.

I HAVE TO TAKE MY ADVANTAGES AS THEY COME, ALL RIGHT?

NATE.

I'M GOING TO GIVE YOU A FIVE-SECOND HEAD START.

AND THEN I'M GOING TO COME AFTER YOU AND *DESTROY YOU*.

ARE YOU KIDDING?

JUST THINK ABOUT THIS FOR A MINUTE! *I BRUISE VERY EASILY!* CHARLIE, YOU'RE GOING TO BE LATE FOR FIRST PERIOD!

ONE.

THEY WERE BOTH LATE FOR FIRST PERIOD.

MR. NOLAN, WHY WERE YOU TRYING TO MAKE MR. HARDING EAT YOUR PHYSICS BOOK?

PRINCIPAL GETTY

I WASN'T TRYING TO MAKE HIM *EAT* IT.

IT'S A MISUNDERSTANDING—

PRINCIPA

HE STOLE A PICTURE OF ME AND HE PHOTOCOPIED IT ONTO A BUNCH OF FLYERS AND CALLED ME A COWARD AND I'M NOT EVEN RUNNING FOR OFFICE!

YOU CAN'T LAUNCH A SMEAR CAMPAIGN AGAINST SOMEBODY WHO'S NOT EVEN RUNNING AGAINST YOU, NATE.

PLEASE, PLEASE EXPEL HIM.

MR. HARDING, TAKE DOWN THE FLYERS. THIS IS SCHOOL POLITICS, NOT U.S. POLITICS.

AS FAR AS WHETHER OR NOT YOU'RE RUNNING FOR STUDENT BODY PRESIDENT, THAT'S SOMETHING YOU'LL HAVE TO CLEAR UP ON YOUR OWN.

WHAT? NO!

ALTHOUGH I HEAR THE CHEERLEADERS HAVE PUT TOGETHER AN IMPRESSIVE RIBBON DRIVE FOR YOU, MR. NOLAN.

THIS IS SO UNFAIR.

IT *IS* SO UNFAIR! I WANT MY OWN CHEERLEADERS!

GET OUT OF MY OFFICE.

SLAM

GAME DAY

LISTEN UP, NOLAN. ARE YOU LISTENING?

YESSIR.

D'YOU KNOW HOW MANY SCRAWNY WHITE BOYS IN THIS SCHOOL WOULD CHEW OFF YOUR LEGS TO GET IN THE TEAM'S STARTING LINEUP?

NO?

THAT'S RIGHT, NOLAN: A LOT.

YAAAA

RAAAAHHH WOOO

'SUP.

HEY.

SO, YOU ACTUALLY AFRAID OF PONIES?

FW ET

72

SMART SHOTS, NOLAN, TAKE SMART SHOTS!

WSST

WIISH

WHAM

YOU OKAY, NOLAN?

YEAH. WHAT'S THE SCORE?

60-61 FOR THEM.

FWIST

WSH

TONK

4:37

HOME   PERIOD   VISITO

62   4   6

GREAT PLA

WE COULD *WIN* THIS THING.

NOLAN! HEAD IN THE *GAME!*

WE'RE AHEAD BY ONE AND THERE ARE 45 SECONDS LEFT IN THE GAME.

WATCH THE TURNOVERS AND KEEP AN EYE OUT FOR WHEN THEY SCREW UP.

WE CAN WIN THIS THING.

YO, GUYS, GROUP HUG!

62 4 63

VOTE FOR A *WINNING* TEAM

VOTE *HARDING* FOR STUDENT BODY PREZ

HE'S DEAD.

FWUMP

SCREECH

HEH!

MR. NOLAN'S OUT OF TOWN. HE CALLED ME TO COME GET CHARLIE.

IT'S A GOOD THING YOU'RE HERE. GOD KNOWS IT TAKES A WINNING TEAM TO TAKE CARE OF A CONCUSSED GUY.

I SEE YOU NOTICED MY NEW CAMPAIGN AD.

I DIDN'T KNOW YOU AND NOLAN KNEW EACH OTHER.

YEAH . . .

YOU—

I'LL—

BLARG

HOW'D YOU GET KNOCKED OUT, ANYWAY?

I THINK I'M GONNA RALPH AGAIN.

DON'T YOU DARE HURL IN MY CAR! I'LL KILL YOU IF YOU HURL IN MY CAR.

YOU'LL KILL ME? *I'LL* KILL *YOU.*

CLACK

SCREECH

LOOK, I'M SORRY I HURT YOUR FEELINGS, BUT THIS ELECTION IS TOO IMPORTANT—

YOU DIDN'T HURT MY *FEELINGS.*

RIGHT, BECAUSE BASKETBALL PLAYERS DON'T HAVE FEELINGS.

FINE, BE LIKE THAT. SEE IF I CARE.

NEXT DAY

SNAP

HIDEOUS WRONGS COMMITTED AGAINST MY PERSON:

	BASKETBALL PLAYERS	CHEERLEADERS	PEOPLE SUCKING UP TO THEM
SHOVED INTO LOCKERS	5	1	2 (!!)

JERK ➤   ◄ ME

TRIPPED IN HALLWAY	1	4	3 (possibly some unintentional, but I DOUBT IT!!!!)

TRIP

PRINCIPAL

YOU KNOW I CAN'T PROVE YOU PUT THAT MESSAGE ON THE SCOREBOARD AT LAST NIGHT'S GAME.

BUT THAT'S NOT THE POINT.

THE POINT IS THE MESSAGE WAS DISLOYAL, UNKIND, AND IN BAD TASTE.

AND I'M SURE WHOEVER PUT IT ON THE SCOREBOARD KNEW THAT.

I HEAR FROM COACH FETZER YOU COLLECTED MR. NOLAN FROM THE HOSPITAL YESTERDAY.

I WANTED TO CHECK IN WITH YOU AND SEE HOW HE WAS DOING.

UH—HE'S FINE, PRINCIPAL GETTY. HE'S DOING OKAY.

HE'S JUST SLEEPING THE REST OF IT OFF TODAY. THE DOCTORS AT THE HOSPITAL SAID HE WAS FINE.

THAT'S GOOD TO HEAR. YOU'RE DISMISSED.

CHCK

ADMINISTRATION

SERIOUSLY, DO YOU WANT THIS GUY FOR SBP? VOTE NOLAN

ENDORSED BY THE HOLLOW RIDGE CHEERLEADERS

HA HA HA HA

THIS MEANS WAR.

NATE, MAYBE YOU SHOULD LET THIS THING GO—

NO! I HAVE TO *WIN*! WE'LL LOSE OUR FUNDING UNLESS I *WIN*!

OKAY, OKAY.

I HAVE A NEW PLAN.

I DON'T LIKE WHERE THIS IS GOING.

ALL I NEED IS A SOURCE FOR INDUSTRIAL WEED KILLER

HI, MOM.

ARE YOU ALL RIGHT? YOUR FATHER CALLED ME AND SAID YOU HAD A CONCUSSION. IS HE THERE WITH YOU?

UH . . . HE'S BUSY.

WELL, IT'S NOT LIKE HE CAN JUST COME HOME FROM A CONFERENCE BECAUSE I FELL DOWN.

HE'S OUT ON BUSINESS, ISN'T HE?

I DON'T CARE IF HE'S NEGOTIATING WORLD PEACE, HE SHOULD COME HOME WHEN HIS SON'S BEEN HURT.

I DON'T SEE YOU DUMPING YOUR OIL SLICK OF A BOYFRIEND AND FLYING OUT HERE FOR ME EITHER.

IT'S NOT A BIG DEAL. I JUST HAD A HEADACHE.

IT IS A BIG DEAL. AND IT'S AN EVEN BIGGER DEAL WHEN MY SON HASN'T BEEN ANSWERING MY PHONE CALLS FOR A MONTH.

I'M GOING TO BE LATE FOR SCHOOL. I'LL TALK TO YOU LATER, OKAY?

CHARLIE, WAIT, WE NEED TO TALK. SOMETHING IMPORTANT—

WHAT'S GOING ON?

WELL! THIS IS AWKWARD.

DON'T LOOK AT ME LIKE THAT. I'M THE ONE GETTING DEFAMED HERE.

ALL FOUR OF YOU CHUCKLEHEADS GET YOUR BUTTS IN MY OFFICE THIS MINUTE.

I ASSUME YOU ALL KNOW WHY YOU'RE HERE.

IF NOT, I CAN SHOW YOU LAST NIGHT'S FOOTAGE FROM A SECURITY CAMERA WE HAD INSTALLED NEXT TO THE FOOTBALL FIELD LAST MONTH.

I SPENT HALF AN HOUR THIS MORNING IN CAUCUS WITH THE SCHOOL BOARD, TRYING TO DECIDE WHAT AN APPROPRIATE PUNISHMENT FOR TRESPASS AND VANDALISM WAS.

PRINCIPAL GETTY

I'M NOT TRYING TO MAKE EXCUSES, PRINCIPAL GETTY.

WHAT WE DID WAS IN EXTREMELY POOR JUDGMENT AND TASTE, BUT WE WERE OBEYING THE SPIRIT OF THE ELECTORAL PROCESS.

WHAT SHE SAID!

CLEARLY WE GOT CARRIED AWAY.

WHAT, YOU DON'T HAVE ANYTHING TO CONTRIBUTE TO THIS ROYAL MESS?

NOPE, BECAUSE I HAD NOTHING TO DO WITH ANY OF THIS.

IS HE TELLING THE TRUTH?

YEAH.

YOU KNOW WHAT, THAT'S IT.

I'M THROUGH WITH YOU GUYS. NO FUNDING FOR THE ROBOTICS COMPETITION—

NO—

—AND NO FUNDING FOR NEW CHEERLEADING UNIFORMS.

PRINCIPAL *GETTY*—!

AND GOOD LUCK EXPLAINING IT TO YOUR TEAMS.

GOD, THIS IS DISGUSTING. I DON'T KNOW HOW PEOPLE CAN DRINK THIS.

I'M SO, SO, SORRYYYYYY.

YOU CAN'T KEEP DRINKING THIS. YOU'RE TALKING TO A PILE OF METAL.

THIS PILE OF METAL, CHARLIE, IS CALLED *THE BEAST.*

AND RIGHT NOW, HE'S *MY ONLY FRIEND.*

I HOPE YOU'RE HAPPY! YOU'VE *RUINED* MY LIFE!

SURE, OKAY, THIS IS MY FAULT.

NATE, I'M GOING TO BREAK YOU IN HALF.

GET OUT OF THE WAY, NOLAN! I NEED TO KILL HIM BEFORE I HAVE SOME KIND OF ASTHMA ATTACK.

Boot

NATE, YOU'RE **DEAD!**

YEAH, YOU'RE ON YOUR OWN FOR THIS ONE.

...OOPS?

BEG FOR IT, AND MAYBE I'LL LET YOU LIVE.

WHAM POW KR—

UH, YOU GUYS GOING TO WANT A TURN POUNDING ON NATE?

NO.

WE'RE HERE TO TELL THEM THERE'S A WAY WE COULD GET AROUND THIS FUNDING THING . . .

. . . BUT WATCHING JOANNA BEAT NATE UP IS KIND OF FUNNY.

WHAM WHAM

HEY, JOANNA?

FWIP

WHAM WHAM WHAM WHAM WHAM

SO THE POINT OF A ROBOT RUMBLE IS THAT THE ROBOTS TEAR EACH OTHER INTO TINY, TINY PIECES?

YESSSS.

JUST TO CLARIFY: YOU *LIKE* THE ROBOT, RIGHT?

WE *LOVE* THE ROBOT.

AND I THINK THIS IS A *TOTALLY STUPID IDEA.*

CAN YOU THINK OF A BETTER IDEA?

NO . . .

BUT WHERE ARE WE GOING TO GET THE MONEY TO SOUP UP THE BEAST?

HE'S NOT A FIGHTING ROBOT.

MAKING HIM READY FOR THAT KIND OF PUNISHMENT IS GOING TO COST.

DO WE KNOW ANYONE SPOILED ENOUGH TO HAVE A CREDIT CARD AND AN UNLIMITED LINE OF CREDIT?

WELL . . .

HOLLY ALWAYS HAD MONEY.

THIS PLACE IS SERIOUSLY FREAKING ME OUT.

THIS WILL *NEVER* WORK.

THIS *HAS* TO WORK.

RIIING

HEH!

RIIING

MOM
CALLING

CLICK

YOU HAVE TO
TALK TO HER
SOMETIME,
YOU KNOW.

I KNOW.

THAT'S NO MOON.

?

IS THERE A REASON YOU LOSERS ARE HERE?

OR ARE YOU JUST OVER TO REVEL IN THE FACT THAT YOU'VE BROUGHT US DOWN WITH YOU?

WE WERE, UH, ACTUALLY GOING TO PROPOSE A COLLABORATION.

YOU KNOW. POOL OUR RESOURCES.

BEAT IT.

YOU SHOULD REALLY HEAR US OUT.

ARE YOU KIDDING ME?? YOU'VE RUINED US FOR COMPETITION!

I'M SORRY, I'VE FORGOTTEN THE PART WHERE I FORCED YOU TO POUR WEED KILLER ON THE FIELD.

HOLLY, IF YOU KILL HIM, YOUR DAD IS DEFINITELY GOING TO TAKE AWAY YOUR CAR.

FINE, WHAT'S THIS PLAN OF YOURS?

WE HAVE A PROPOSITION. AND IT MIGHT SAVE ALL OUR ASSES.

THEREFORE, INVEST IN *THE BEAST.*

THE BEAST IS THE ANSWER TO OUR PROBLEMS.

DON'T YOU SEE? THIS IS OUR ONLY HOPE.

LOOK, YOU MAKE AN INVESTMENT TO GET US TO THE ROBOT RUMBLE, AND WE'LL SHARE WHAT WE WIN. YOU GET YOUR UNIFORMS AND WE GET OUR FUNDING TO GO TO THE NATIONALS, PLUS YOU CLEAR AN EXTRA $3,000. THERE'S NO WAY TO LOSE.

UNLESS YOU LOSE THE ROBOT RUMBLE.

WE WON'T LOSE.

THIS IS A MAJOR RISK. IF WE AGREE, WE'D HAVE CONDITIONS.

WHATEVER YOU WANT.

THAT'S GOOD, BECAUSE CONDITION NUMBER ONE IS WE ACCOMPANY YOU TO THE ROBOT RUMBLE. TO KEEP AN EYE ON OUR INVESTMENT.

DO WE HAVE A DEAL?

YES.

CONGRATS.

WE'RE NOW OFFICIALLY PARTNERS.

SO NOW WHAT?

NOW WE GO SHOPPING.

OKAY, WE HAVE LESS THAN TWO WEEKS TO TURN A ROBOT THAT PICKS THINGS UP INTO A ROBOT THAT *KILLS OTHER ROBOTS.*

CHAINSAWS, PEOPLE, WE NEED CHAINSAWS!

HELLO?

CHARLES LANE NOLAN, IF YOU SO MUCH AS THINK ABOUT HANGING UP ON ME, I WILL FLY OUT THERE AND HAND YOU YOUR REAR END ON A PLATTER. AM I UNDERSTOOD?

WHAT IS IT, MOM?

YOU'VE BEEN IGNORING MY PHONE CALLS FOR WEEKS! I CAN'T REMEMBER THE LAST TIME YOU SAID MORE THAN TWO SENTENCES TO ME—

I'VE BEEN BUSY.

THE BUDGET DOES NOT INCLUDE DELUXE CHAINSAWS, HARDING!

MOM, SERIOUSLY, I'M IN THE MIDDLE OF SOMETHING IMPORTANT.

YOUR FAMILY ISN'T IMPORTANT?

CHARLIE, TIM'S ASKED ME TO MARRY HIM.

I WAS HOPING YOU'D BE HAPPY FOR ME . . .

I THOUGHT YOU WERE SUPPOSED TO BE HAPPY WITH *US*.

OKAY, SO HOLLY'S BEING A PAIN ABOUT THE CHAINSAWS, BUT CHECK OUT THIS *BLOWTORCH*. COOL, HUH?

YOU OKAY?

YEAH. LET'S WELD THE CRAP OUT OF THIS THING.

IF WE WEIGHED DOWN THE BACK OF THE BEAST, IT COULD HANDLE EXTRA WEIGHT UP FRONT.

LIKE THE WEIGHT OF A CHAINSAW.

I DON'T KNOW. I DON'T THINK JUST ATTACHING A CHAINSAW BLADE IS GOING TO WORK.

ANYTHING I CAN DO?

NO, CHARLIE, THIS IS ROBOTICS CLUB ONLY STUFF.

ARE YOU AN EXPERT AT ROBOTICS, LIKE ME? NO, YOU PLAY BASKETBALL.

I GUESS, BUT EVEN I CAN SEE IF YOU WEIGH DOWN THE BACK OF THE BEAST TO COUNTER-BALANCE A CHAINSAW, YOU'RE GOING TO KILL ITS SPEED.

JAPAN

INSTEAD OF ATTACHING A CHAINSAW, WHY DON'T YOU JUST EDGE THE BEAST WITH CHAINSAW TEETH?

LOOKS GOOD, HUH?

IT'S GOOD, BUT—

—IT NEEDS A LITTLE SOMETHING *EXTRA*.

THAT COUCH IN THE BASEMENT, THINK WE CAN STRIP IT FOR PARTS?

PERFECT!

YEAH, *PERFECT.*

OKAY.

LADIES AND GENTLEMEN,

HOLD ON TO YOUR BUTTS.

HEH!

VREEEE

KRAK

OH CRAP. WE APPEAR TO HAVE ANGERED IT.

NVRREE

NATE, TURN IT OFF TURN IT OFF TURN IT OFF!

BASH

SCREECH

PURRRRRRR

OKAY, THAT WAS KIND OF AWESOME.

THAT EVENING

THE DISTANCE ATTACK MECHANISM IS WORKING OUT BETTER THAN WE THOUGHT.

YEAH, THE CHAINSAW IDEA PANNED OUT.

RIING

HELLO?

THIS SOLDERING IS HORRIBLE. IT'S GOING TO BLOW APART ON IMPACT.

IT'S A ROBOT, NOT AN ACTION MOVIE.

IS THIS CHARLIE NOLAN?

YES, THIS IS HE.

CHARLIE, THIS MIGHT NOT BE A GOOD TIME, BUT I WANTED TO GET IN TOUCH WITH YOU.

UM, SORRY, WHO IS THIS? I DON'T RECOGNIZE THE NUMBER.

NOW—DON'T HANG UP, BECAUSE YOUR MOTHER SAYS YOU'RE REALLY FOND OF THAT—

OH MY GOD. YOU'RE— YOU'RE MY MOM'S *BOYFRIEND.* WHY ARE YOU *CALLING* ME?

I JUST WANTED AN OPPORTUNITY TO TALK TO YOU, CHARLIE. YOUR BEHAVIOR THESE PAST FEW WEEKS HAS REALLY HURT GINA'S FEELINGS, AND AS SOMEBODY WHO'S GOING TO BE A PART OF HER LIFE NOW, I THOUGHT THAT WE—

MY "BEHAVIOR"? MY "BEHAVIOR"? YOU KNOW WHAT—

YOU CAN JUST BITE ME!

UM . . . WANT TO SEE THE IMPROVEMENTS WE'VE MADE?

SURE.

155

THE ROBOT RUMBLE WINNER LAST YEAR WAS A BOT NOT DISSIMILAR TO OURS—

IT WAS SMALL, DOMED, AND IT ALSO HAD A FREAKING GIANT SPIKE ON THE END OF A LONG METAL ROD.

THE SPIKE WORKS UP AND DOWN, AND CENTRIPETAL FORCE ROTATES IT AROUND THE BOT.

WITH THE SPIKE WE CAN ATTACK FROM A DISTANCE AND RISK LESS DAMAGE TO THE BEAST. NEAT, HUH?

YEAH, VERY NEAT.

THANKS CHARLIE. I GUESS YOU'RE KIND OF COOL.

SHE THOUGHT I WASN'T COOL?

OH MY GOD, SOMEBODY THOUGHT YOU WEREN'T COOL, THE WORLD IS COMING TO AN END.

NEXT DAY, BASKETBALL PRACTICE

SERIOUSLY, COACH, IF WE'RE ALL TOO BROKEN TO PLAY, YOU KNOW WE CAN'T WIN, RIGHT?

WALK IT OFF, BOYS.

WHAT THE HELL?

MR. NOLAN'S GOING TO *LOVE* THIS.

HEY, HAVE YOU SEEN CHARLIE?

WHO'S CHARLIE?

YOU ARE AWARE YOU'RE THROWING THE BIGGEST PARTY OF THE YEAR DOWNSTAIRS, RIGHT?

NOT ON PURPOSE!

I TOLD THE GUYS TO MEET AT MY PLACE FOR *PIZZA*.

NOT INVITE HALF THE SCHOOL TO BRING OVER THEIR PARENTS' CHEAP ALCOHOL AND GET DRUNK ON MY FRONT LAWN.

YOU REALLY ARE THE WORST COOL KID EVER.

WHATEVER. IT DOESN'T MATTER. THE ONLY WAY THIS COULD BLOW UP ON ME IS IF MY DAD SHOWED UP.

WHICH HE NEVER DOES.

YEAH, I CAN JUST IMAGINE WHAT HE'D SAY IF HE CAME HOME RIGHT NOW.

CRASH

DAD. YOU'RE HOME EARLY.

IF YOU HADN'T COME HOME A DAY EARLY, YOU WOULDN'T EVEN KNOW!

HOW DOES THAT EXCUSE YOU THROWING A *KEGGER* WHILE I'M NOT HOME?

THERE WASN'T EVEN A *KEG!* AND WHY DO YOU CARE?

CHARLES LANE NOLAN, I AM YOUR *FATHER*–

–AND AS LONG AS YOU LIVE UNDER THIS ROOF, I AM THE *BOSS OF YOU*–

YOU?? WHAT A *JOKE!*

YOU'RE NEVER HOME! AND WHEN YOU ARE YOU MAKE ME GO ON ALL THOSE *STUPID* CAMPING TRIPS–

THAT'S IT! YOU'RE GROUNDED! TWO MONTHS!

NEXT DAY

HEY.

POINK

HEY. C'MON, LOOK UP, YOU FREAK.

POINK

NATE, SERIOUSLY, LAY OFF.

HOW'D IT GO WITH YOUR DAD?

HE WAS LOUDER THAN THE *PARTY* WAS. LET'S NOT PRETEND YOU COULDN'T HEAR EVERY WORD.

HEH.

HOW LONG ARE YOU GROUNDED FOR? BECAUSE WE KINDA STILL NEED YOUR HELP WITH THE BEAST—

TWO MONTHS.

BUT DON'T WORRY! I MANAGED TO CONVINCE HIM WORKING ON THE ROBOT WILL KEEP ME OUT OF TROUBLE!

SO YOU WON'T BE WITHOUT MY AWESOME WELDING SKILLS FOR A SINGLE SECOND.

YOU DO KNOW THIS WASN'T MY FAULT, RIGHT?

YES, NATE, I KNOW.

RIING

HELLO?

WHERE ARE YOU?

NATE, IT'S 7:30 IN THE MORNING. WHY ARE YOU AWAKE?

THE CHEERLEADERS, CHARLIE—THEY CALLED ME HALF AN HOUR AGO. THEY'RE ON THEIR WAY. THEY WANT A "STATUS REPORT."

175

I THOUGHT YOU SAID THE BEAST WAS ALMOST READY.

THE BEAST *IS* ALMOST READY, BUT THAT'S NOT WHY I'M CALLING.

WHY *ARE* YOU CALLING, THEN?

BECAUSE I THINK I HEARD YOUR DAD INVITE YOUR MOTHER TO THANKSGIVING DINNER.

ARE YOU IN THE BATHROOM OR SOMETHING? I HEAR WATER.

177

ARE YOU SURE YOU HEARD MY DAD RIGHT?

I SWEAR—HE'S, LIKE, OUT ON YOUR BACK PORCH TALKING TO HER ON HIS CELL PHONE—

—PROBABLY HIDING OUT THERE SO HE WON'T WAKE YOU UP.

NATE, ARE YOU *SURE*?

MAN, I'M, LIKE, HIDING UNDERNEATH YOUR DECK AT THIS POINT! SHUT UP SO I CAN HEAR MORE CLEARLY.

OKAY, SO IT SOUNDS LIKE NOW THEY'RE TRYING TO FIGURE OUT WHEN SHE SHOULD COME OVER.

AND—OH GEEZ— IF SHE SHOULD BRING HER FIANCÉ.

UM, OKAY, YOUR DAD IS SAYING THAT'S PROBABLY A BAD IDEA, BUT IT SEEMS SHE'S FIGHTING HIM ON THAT AND NOW HE'S GONE KINDA QUIET—

—AND I CAN'T HEAR WHAT THEY'RE SAYING ANYMORE—

—AND, UM—THAT WOULD BE BECAUSE HE'S DOWN HERE GLARING AT ME INSTEAD.

BEAUTIFUL DAY, ISN'T IT, MR. NOLAN! THE VIEW FROM UNDER HERE IS JUST—OKAY! OKAY! I'M HANGING UP ALREADY!

CLICK

179

SEE? HE'S NOT SAWING AT HIS WRISTS. CAN I GO HOME NOW?

YES, BUT WE'RE GOING TO TALK ABOUT YOU BEING A BAD INFLUENCE ONE DAY.

OH SURE, BECAUSE YOU AND THE EX-MRS. NOLAN MAKING HIM CRAZY IS MY FAULT.

UH. GOTTA RUN.

SHOOM

BOMB

CHARLIE. YOUR MOTHER WANTS TO SEE YOU. I THINK, BECAUSE SHE'S YOUR MOTHER, YOU SHOULD SEE HER TOO.

SURE. FINE. WHATEVER.

I'M GLAD YOU AND MOM HAVE SUCH A GREAT DIVORCE.

CHARLIE, WE NEED TO TALK ABOUT THIS. IT HAS BEEN A VERY BAD YEAR FOR US AND—

THIS HAS NOT BEEN A "VERY BAD YEAR FOR US." THIS HAS BEEN, LIKE, THE *FIFTH* BAD YEAR IN A ROW.

EXCUSE ME?

I *DIDN'T* WANT YOU AND MOM TO GET DIVORCED, I *DIDN'T* WANT HER TO MOVE TO CALIFORNIA, I *DIDN'T* WANT HER TO GET A *FIANCÉ*, AND I *DON'T* WANT THEM AT THANKSGIVING!

UM.

AND ALSO, I DON'T WANT TO GO CAMPING *EVER AGAIN.*

IT ALWAYS RAINS AND THE SHOWERS SMELL AND THEN I COME HOME WITH SOME KIND OF *FUNGUS* GROWING ON MY SOCKS.

WHY CAN'T WE JUST STAY HOME AND WATCH TV LIKE NORMAL PEOPLE?

I LIKE TV. IT'S *INDOORS.*

AND I FELL IN THE CREEK AND I THINK THERE'S FISH IN MY BOXERS SO I'M GOING TO GO UPSTAIRS AND CHANGE MY PANTS NOW!

OKAY. I'M GLAD WE HAD THIS TALK.

WHAT DO YOU WANT ME TO SAY? HE'S MADE HIS OPINION ABOUT THIS THANKSGIVING THING PERFECTLY CLEAR.

WOW, YOU MIGHT ACTUALLY PULL THIS OFF.

YOUR CONFIDENCE OVERWHELMS ME.

HOW'S THE INVESTOR MEETING GOING?

I THINK SHE LIKES IT.

AT LEAST WE KNOW IT CAN KILL INDISCRIMINATELY.

THAT WAS THE *POINT*, RIGHT? THAT'S HOW YOU WIN THE ROBOT RUMBLE? BY KILLING THE OTHER ROBOTS?

Y-YES.

VRRRRRR

THEN YES, I LIKE IT.

HE'S A GREAT ROBOT.

HE'S THE *BEST* ROBOT.

HAVE WE THOUGHT ABOUT HOW WE'RE GETTING TO THE RUMBLE?

IN MY CAR I CAN DRIVE.

NATE, WE HAVE EIGHT PEOPLE GOING TO THE ROBOT RUMBLE, AND THERE'S NO WAY THE BEAST WILL FIT IN YOUR TRUNK.

OKAY, SO HOW CAN WE GET THERE?

WE TAKE MY DAD'S SUV.

IT SEATS EIGHT AND IT HAS ENOUGH ROOM IN THE BACK FOR A DOZEN ROBOTS.

BUT . . . CHARLIE, THAT'S YOUR **DAD'S** CAR.

SO? I KNOW WHERE HE KEEPS THE KEYS.

THE ROBOT RUMBLE IS ON THANKSGIVING.

DON'T YOU . . . Y'KNOW, WANT TO SPEND THANKSGIVING WITH YOUR FAMILY?

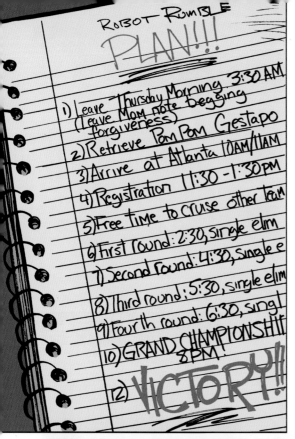

ROBOT RUMBLE
PLAN!!!

1) Leave - Thursday Morning. 3:30 AM
   (Leave Mom note begging forgiveness)
2) Retrieve Pom Pom Gestapo
3) Arrive at Atlanta 10AM/11AM
4) Registration 11:30 - 1:30PM
5) Free time to cruise other team
6) First round: 2:30, single elim
7) Second round: 4:30, single e
8) Third round: 5:30, single elim
9) Fourth round: 6:30, singl
10) GRAND CHAMPIONSHIP
    8PM!
12) VICTORY!!

WE'VE GOT TO PICK UP THE CHEERLEADERS.

LET'S GO.

ARGUE VOCIFEROUSLY ABOUT BEST WAY
TO GET ONTO THE HIGHWAY, 15 MIN.

HOLLOW RIDGE

GET INTO A SELF-DEFEATING ARGUMENT ABOUT
UNFAIR GENDER STEREOTYPES THAT ENDS WITH
HOLLY THREATENING TO GIVE EVERYBODY A
TASTE OF HER FIERCE, SWIFT JUSTICE, 45 MIN.

UM, I MEANT TO THANK YOU. I MEAN, FOR DRIVING US TO ATLANTA.

IT WAS BETTER THAN THE OTHER OPTION.

I'M SORRY, I'M SORRY, I'M SORRY, I KNOW IT'S THANKSGIVING AND EVERYTHING, I'M SORRY—

CLACK

BIP

CLACK

BRIING 'RING

RING

CLICK

YOU SURE YOU WANT TO DO THAT?

PLEASE, I GAVE UP TALKING TO THEM YEARS AGO.

WHOA.

YOU GUYS GO REGISTER US, AND GET BADGES FOR EVERYBODY—WE NEED EIGHT.

AND HOW'S OUR ROBOT?

SO PRETTY! THE PRETTIEST ROBOT OF THEM ALL.

VRRR

YEAH, OKAY. THE ROBOT IS PRETTY.

GOD, I HOPE THIS WORKS.

RRRRMM

HEH.

FOOOM

FWIP

AND HERE'S OUR HOME FOR THE DURATION OF THE COMPETITION.

WELL, I GUESS IT'S A STEP UP FROM YOUR BASEMENT.

SHUT UP. MY BASEMENT IS *AWESOME*.

OMMMMM... OMM MMM

OOOHMMMMMM

ARE THEY *CHANTING?*

YEP. TO CTHULHU, APPARENTLY.

IT'S A WHOLE DIFFERENT BREED OF NERD HERE.

YEP.

I REGISTERED THE TEAM.

WE ALSO MET THESE GUYS.

HELLO! CHIP CLYDESDALE OF CHANNEL 11 NEWS! HOW DOES IT FEEL TO BE THE YOUNGEST TEAM OF COMPETITORS AT THE ROBOT RUMBLE?

FWISH

UM . . . OKAY, I GUESS.

AND HOW DO YOU FEEL ABOUT *TEAM AWESOME'S* CHANCES IN THE COMPETITION?

WAIT... HOLLY, YOU NAMED THE TEAM *WHAT*?

NOBODY TOLD ME WE HAD TO HAVE A NAME! IT'S ALL I COULD THINK OF.

TEAM AWESOME IS GOING TO KICK ROBOT ASS AT THE ROBOT RUMBLE.

ERRAAGH. *FINE.*

YAY! WE'RE TEAM AWESOME!

SHUT UP, BEN.

SFSSSSHH

SCREEE

FWUMP

NO NO NO NO. NATE, WE ARE NOT LETTING OUR BABY GO IN THAT RING. HE'LL BE *DESTROYED.*

JOANNA . . .

THE BEAST WILL BE OKAY. HE'S THE BEST ROBOT.

HE *IS* THE BEST ROBOT.

LET'S DO THIS.

216

217

I CAN'T BELIEVE YOU'RE NOT DRIVING THE ROBOT.

ARE YOU KIDDING? IF I TRIED TO DRIVE THE BOT IN COMPETITION I'D HAVE A SEIZURE AND DIE.

BESIDES, JOANNA HAS A *GIFT*.

NO MERCY. NOT NOW, NOT EVER.

FOLKS, UNPRECEDENTED FRESHMAN TEAM AWESOME HAS DEFEATED TEAM AGENT ORANGE IN A STUNNING UPSET!

SSSSS

YABBA A HA A

WE . . . WON?

BLARG

NATE, EW.

HOW'RE THE REPAIRS COMING?

GOOD! PRETTY MUCH DONE.

WE MADE OURSELVES A TOUGH LITTLE ROBOT.

NEXT UP WE'RE FIGHTING TEAM SHUFFLE YOUR FEET. THEIR ROBOT MADE IT TO THE FINALS LAST YEAR.

ANY TIPS FOR FIGHTING THEM?

MOVE FAST, I GUESS. THEIR ROBOT'S SUPPOSED TO BE ONE OF THE BEST.

DOOOOM

Squee Squee

Squee Squee

KRUNCH

FHSSHH

WOW.

NOT SO TOUGH AFTER ALL.

IF I WERE TEAM SHUFFLE YOUR FEET, I DON'T THINK I'D SHOW MY FACE AT ANY KIND OF ROBOT-RELATED EVENT FOR THE NEXT COUPLE YEARS.

TEAM ROCK OPERA. THEY'RE LAST YEAR'S CHAMPS, AND THEIR ROBOT IS NAMED POST-MODERN ENNUI.

I WAS *EMBARRASSED* FOR THEM. REALLY, REALLY EMBARRASSED.

WHO NAMES A ROBOT POST-MODERN ENNUI?

JERKS.

WHO ARE WE UP AGAINST NEXT?

OH, MAN, WE'D HEARD OUR COMPETITION WAS CONSORTING WITH OUR COLLECTIVE ENEMY, BUT . . .

BUT WE WERE HOPING YOU HAD MORE HONOR THAN THAT.

EXCEPT . . .

THAT'S REAL.

GENUINE.

100 PERCENT.

JOCK.

EXCUSE ME?

WE DON'T LIKE YOUR KIND HERE AT THE RUMBLE.

YOUR KIND ISN'T WELCOME.

WHO **ARE** YOU?

WE'RE TEAM ROCK OPERA.

WE'RE GOING TO KICK YOUR JOCK ROBOT'S **ASS.**

BECAUSE HERE AT THE ROBOT RUMBLE—

—NERDS ARE **KING.**

CHARLIE. C'MON AND HELP US WITH THE BEAST.

OOOH, LOOK AT THE LITTLE NERD, TRAITOR TO HIS PEOPLE.

HOW MANY TIMES DID THIS JOCK SHOVE YOUR HEAD IN A TOILET, *TRAITOR*?

LAY OFF MY TEAM, GUYS.

SHYEAH, RIGHT.

LOOK AT *THIS*. THEY EVEN BROUGHT A *GIRL*.

NO GIRLS ALLOWED AT THE ROBOT RUMBLE, YOU—

AHHHHH

FHUMP

OWOWOWOW! C'MON MAN, THAT HUUUURRTS!

CHARLIE, STOP.

Ow Ow Ow

WE'LL MEET THEM ON THE BATTLEFIELD.

AND WE'LL BE THE ONES TAKING YOUR ROBOT APART, PIECE BY PIECE.

HEY, DID YOU NOTICE SOMETHING WEIRD ABOUT THE DESIGN OF THAT ROBOT?

SAY, IN THEORY, YOU COULD *FLIP* IT.

YOU CAN'T FLIP IT! THE THING PROBABLY HAS A BRICK AT THE BOTTOM! IT'S WEIGHTED TO STAY UPRIGHT.

DOOOM

I DON'T NEED TO FLIP IT *OVER*.

I JUST NEED IT TO *FLIP*.

HOW ARE *FLIP OVER* AND AND *FLIP* MATERIALLY DIFFERENT AT—OH MY GOD, I CAN'T BELIEVE WE'RE IN THE SEMIFINALS AND I'M ARGUING *SEMANTICS* WITH YOU.

243

TURN AND FACE ME!

VIIP

SHOOO

RRRM

THIS IS A STUPID PLAN, JOANNA!

NO BACKSEAT DRIVING.

VR

I CAN'T BELIEVE IT! WE'RE ONE FIGHT AWAY FROM *WINNING* THIS THING!

OH MY GOD, $10,000! WE'RE GOING TO WIN $10,000!

THAT WAS SOME BADASS DRIVING, JOANNA.

THANKS, CHARLIE.

I REALLY THINK WE CAN WIN THIS THING.

WE CAN TOTALLY WIN.

NOTHING CAN STOP US.

WE . . .
LOST.

THUD

IT'S ALL RIGHT, JO, YOU CAN FIX IT.

YOU DID AMAZING.

YOU DID THE BEST YOU COULD, NATE.

AND WE *LOST*.

WE LOST *AND* MY PARENTS ARE GOING TO KILL ME. I DISAPPEARED ON *THANKSGIVING*.

FWUMP

THAT FLOOR IS PRETTY DIRTY.

I DON'T CARE. MY LIFE IS RUINED.

HEY, DIDN'T WE COME IN SECOND?

FIRST LOSER, YES.

GUYS, YOU DID IT.

WHAT, LOST?

NO, YOU MORONS.

YOU *DID* IT!

ACCORDING TO YOUR PLAN, YOU JUST HAD TO COME IN FIRST OR SECOND TO WIN ENOUGH PRIZE MONEY, RIGHT?

YOU DID IT! YOU CAME IN SECOND!

OH MY GOD.

WE . . . DID IT?

YEAH, NATE.

WE'RE GOING TO THE NATIONAL ROBOTICS FAIR!

WE'RE GETTING NEW UNIFORMS!

WE . . . DID IT.

WHUMP

HEY, YOU'RE AWAKE.

CHARLIE.

YEAH?

THANKS FOR DRIVING US TO ATLANTA.

NO PROBLEM.

THIS FLOOR IS REALLY GROSS.

YEAH, YOU SHOULD GET UP.

CHARLIE!

HI, MOM.

YOU RAN AWAY FROM HOME ON *THANKSGIVING*−!

I DON'T THINK SCREAMING AT HIM IS GOING TO BE ALL THAT PRODUCTIVE AT THIS POINT, GINA.

ARE YOU KIDDING ME??

I'M JUST SAYING HE DIDN'T SEEM ALL THAT INCLINED TO STEAL THE CAR AND RUN BEFORE YOU SAID YOU WERE COMING HOME WITH TIM.

HOW WOULD YOU KNOW? YOU WEREN'T EVEN THERE FOR HIS HEAD INJURY!

AND THAT'S *SO MUCH WORSE* THAN NOT BEING HERE FOR THE LAST *FOUR YEARS* OF HIS LIFE?

WILL BOTH OF YOU JUST SHUT UP?

CHARLIE, LOOK, I'M SORRY.

YEAH, FOR WHAT? WHAT ARE YOU SORRY ABOUT?

I MEAN, ARE YOU SORRY FOR BRINGING TIM TO THANKSGIVING? OR ARE YOU SORRY ABOUT MOVING TO SAN DIEGO?

OR ARE YOU SORRY ABOUT THE CURRENT STATE OF SOCIAL SECURITY? ABOUT GLOBAL WARMING? WHAT?

YOU'RE UPSET I MOVED TO SAN DIEGO?

LOOK, WE PROBABLY NEED TO TALK ABOUT THIS SOMEWHERE WE'RE ALL COMFORTABLE. WHY DON'T WE TAKE A BREAK AND TOMORROW WE CAN PLAN A—

WE'RE NOT GOING CAMPING.

WHAT? I THOUGHT YOU GUYS LOVED CAMPING!

WE HATED CAMPING.

BUT YOU GUYS NEVER SAID ANYTHING.

I SAY STUFF ALL THE TIME. YOU JUST NEVER REALLY LISTENED TO ME.

CHARLIE, WHY ARE YOU HERE?

WELL, NATE NEEDED A RIDE.

SO TIM AND I HAD NOTHING TO DO WITH IT?

FWIP FWIP

HEH.

THAT MIGHT HAVE PLAYED A PART IN MY CHOICE, YES.

CHARLIE, WHAT YOU DID WASN'T OKAY, AND WE NEED TO TALK LATER,

BUT YOU'RE THE MOST IMPORTANT THING IN MY LIFE, AND NO MATTER WHAT IT IS, WE CAN WORK IT OUT. OKAY?

OKAY. WHATEVER.

HEY, HOW'D YOU GUYS FIND US, ANYWAY?

WE SAW YOU IDIOTS ON TELEVISION, BEING INTERVIEWED BY CHANNEL 11 NEWS.

SO WE'RE NOT IN TROUBLE ANYMORE, RIGHT?

YEAH, RIGHT. YOU'RE BOTH GROUNDED UNTIL YOU GRADUATE HIGH SCHOOL.

WAIT—WAIT A MINUTE! YOU GUYS CAN'T **GROUND** ME! I'M NOT EVEN YOUR KID!

WATCH US.

PARTS

LOOK AT IT THIS WAY:

THE CHEERLEADERS AREN'T GOING TO BE NAKED, AND YOU'RE GOING TO THE NATIONAL ROBOTICS COMPETITION. WHAT MORE COULD YOU ASK FOR, RIGHT?

THREE WEEKS LATER

HOLLOW RIDGE HIGH SCHOOL

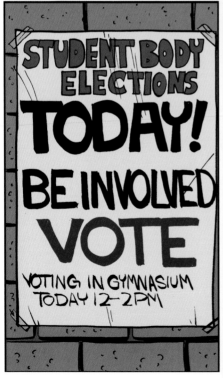

STUDENT BODY ELECTIONS

TODAY!

BE INVOLVED

VOTE

VOTING IN GYMNASIUM TODAY 12-2PM

SO DID YOU VOTE FOR ME?

FOR THE SAKE OF THE SCHOOL, NATE, I VOTED FOR SOMEONE ELSE.

YOU VOTED FOR YOUR **BOYFRIEND**, DIDN'T YOU? DESPITE THE FACT THAT I'M **CLEARLY** A SUPERIOR CANDIDATE!

HE'S NOT MY BOYFRIEND. WE'RE FRIENDS.

WHY DO YOU STILL CARE ABOUT THE ELECTIONS? THE POINT OF YOU WINNING WAS TO GET MONEY FOR THE ROBOTICS COMPETITION. NOW THAT WE **HAVE** MONEY, THE ELECTION DOESN'T MATTER.

WELL, MAYBE I SUDDENLY DISCOVERED A PASSION FOR POLITICS.

HEY.

SO NATE APPARENTLY **STILL** WANTS TO BE STUDENT BODY PRESIDENT.

I HAVE **GREAT** IDEAS THAT COULD IMPROVE THIS SCHOOL!

YEAH? LIKE WHAT?

WELL . . . LIKE, YOU KNOW . . . TAXES . . . AND JOBS? PEOPLE LIKE JOBS.

THE VOTES FROM THE ELECTION HAVE BEEN COUNTED, AND YOUR NEW STUDENT BODY PRESIDENTS ARE—

GARY AND JAKE MORIARTY, IN A LANDSLIDE VICTORY!

EEX-CELLENT.

IT WAS SMART OF US TO APPEAL TO THE HIGH SCHOOL PERVERT VOTE.

YES, THAT DEMOGRAPHIC IS VERY CONSCIENTIOUS ABOUT VOTING.

ALTHOUGH I'M NOT REALLY SURE HOW WE'RE GOING TO MAKE GOOD ON OUR MANDATORY MINI-SKIRTS PROMISE...

WE'LL FIND A WAY.

Y'KNOW, I NEVER KNEW THOSE GUYS' NAMES UNTIL NOW.

OH MY GOD, WE ARE *DOOMED.*

MAYBE NEXT YEAR WE COULD RUN FOR STUDENT BODY PRESIDENT TOGETHER. YOU COULD BE MY VP.

WHY DO *I* HAVE TO BE THE VP?? *CLEARLY* I'M MORE SUITED FOR A LEADERSHIP ROLE.

YOU'D VOTE FOR A HARDING/NOLAN TICKET BEFORE A NOLAN/HARDING ONE, WOULDN'T YOU?

I'D VOTE FOR ANYONE OVER GARY AND JAKE.

WE'VE GOT ONE VOTE, THEN.

ACKNOWLEDGMENTS

Enormous thanks go to Diana Fox, who took a chance on me, as did Calista Brill, Gina Gagliano, and the rest of the talented crew at First Second. Also, there cannot be enough effusive adjectives for Faith, whose art breathed laughter into these characters.

Thanks also to my friends, who though spread across three continents in a multitude of countries, always had time for my panic attacks, thought experiments about driving sort-of-stolen SUVs, and routinely let me sleep on their couches.

Lastly, I am endlessly grateful to the poor souls who had the misfortune of teaching me through the years: Mrs. Thorsen, who let a twelve-year-old make mosaics; Mr. Dickerson, who proved me wrong about science fiction; and Mrs. Nelson, because when I told her I was going to law school, she laughed and said, "No, you're not. You're going to be a writer."

—Prudence Shen

As always, thanks to the First Second elite literary ninja squad: Calista Brill, Gina Gagliano, Colleen AF Venable, Mark Siegel; my awesome agent Bernadette; Prudence, for being totally cool with me transforming a word book into a picture book; the Saturday coffee shop sketch group: Noreen, Mitch, Miriam, Andrew, Ben, Joe, and Tony (sometimes); and Tim. 'Cause he's the best.

—Faith Erin Hicks